WAKE UP, DAD!

Sally Grindley

Illustrated by Siobhan Dodds

DOUBLEDAY

NEW YORK LONDON TORONTO SYDNEY AUCKLAND

Published by Doubleday, a division of
Bantam Doubleday Dell Publishing Group, Inc.
666 Fifth Avenue, New York, New York 10103

Doubleday and the portrayal of an anchor with a dolphin
are trademarks of Doubleday, a division of
Bantam Doubleday Dell Publishing Group, Inc.

Library of Congress Cataloging-in-Publication Data
Grindley, Sally
Wake up, dad!
Summary: A little girl's valiant efforts to rouse
one of her parents early in the morning are firmly
resisted, until she decides joining them in bed will
be lovely and warm.
[1. Morning—Fiction. 2. Parent and child—Fiction.
3. Family life—Fiction] I. Dodds, Siobhan, ill. II. Title.
PZ.7G88446Wak 1989   [E]   88-20386

ISBN 0-385-26017-2 (Trade)
0-385-26018-0 (Library)

"Dad . . . Are you asleep, Dad?"

"Are you asleep, Dad?"

"It's morning, Dad. Look, it's light outside. I've been awake for ages and ages. So has Teddy."

"Wake up, Dad."

"I can tell you what time it is if you want
me to. The big hand is pointing to seven
and the little hand is pointing to six."

"Wake up, Dad."

"Will you mend my truck for me, Dad?
Look, the wheel's come off and it won't
roll. The bell's gone funny too, listen."

"Do you know what Johnny did yesterday? He pulled my hair like this, really hard, and he wouldn't say sorry. He should say sorry, shouldn't he, Dad? I don't like him anymore."

"Can we go to the zoo today, Dad? You said we could go soon. I want to see the gorillas. They're my favorite. They bang on their chests like this, and make a noise like this – AAH-OOOO-AAAH!"

"Wake up, Dad."

"Dad, there's a big spider on the floor.
It's right by your shoes. Do spiders go
into shoes? They could build their nests
in them, couldn't they, Dad?"

"Watch this, Dad!
I can do cartwheels."

"I can do somersaults too.
  Backward ones and forward ones."

"I think Yum-Yum wants to come in,
Dad. She must want her breakfast. Shall
I let her in?
Here she is, Dad. She's come to say
good morning, haven't you, Yum-Yum?"

"She caught a mouse yesterday, Dad, but when she tried to get through the cat-flap she dropped it and it ran away."

"Wake up, Dad."

"Shall I go and get my recorder, Dad? I can nearly play a tune on it."

NO!

"Dad, I'm cold, Dad. Can I get into bed with you?"

"It's lovely and warm in here, isn't it?
Why don't we all go back to sleep?"

"Miaow!"